THIS CANDLEWICK BOOK BELONGS TO:

_____

_____

_____

*To Faye Theresa,*
*my "great" niece*
*T. C.*

First U.S. paperback edition in this format 2008

The Library of Congress has cataloged the hardcover edition as follows:

Cooke, Trish.
So much / Trish Cooke ; illustrated by Helen Oxenbury. —1st U.S. ed.
Summary: Relatives arriving in succession give in to their desire
to squeeze and kiss and play with the baby.
ISBN 978-1-56402-344-5 (hardcover)
[1. Babies—Fiction. 2. Blacks—England—Fiction.]
I. Oxenbury, Helen, ill. II. Title.
PZ7.C77494So 1994
[E]—dc20      94-13435

ISBN 978-0-7636-0296-3 (paperback)
ISBN 978-0-7636-4091-0 (reformatted paperback)

16 APS 11

Printed in Humen, Dongguan, China

This book was typeset in StempelSchneidler.
The illustrations were done in gouache.

Candlewick Press
99 Dover Street
Somerville, Massachusetts 02144

visit us at www.candlewick.com

# So Much!

**Trish Cooke**

**ILLUSTRATED BY**
**Helen Oxenbury**

CANDLEWICK PRESS

They weren't doing anything,
Mom and the baby,
nothing really . . .
Then,
DING DONG!
"Oooooooh!"

Mom looked at the door,
the baby looked at Mom.
It was . . .

Auntie—
Auntie Bibba.
Auntie Bibba came inside with her
arms out wide, wide, wide
and one big, big smile.

"Oooooooh!" she said.
"I want to squeeze him,
 I want to squeeze the baby,
 I want to squeeze him
 SO MUCH!"

And she sat the baby
on her knee
to play clap-clap,
stamp your foot.
Then she read him a book.
"Mmmmmmm . . ."

They weren't doing anything,
Mom and the baby and Auntie Bibba,
nothing really . . .

Then,
DING DONG!
"Hello, hello!"

Mom looked at the door,
Auntie Bibba looked at the baby,
the baby looked at Mom.
It was . . .

Uncle—
Uncle Didi.
Uncle Didi came inside
with his eyebrows
raise high, high, high
and his lips scrunch up
small, small, small.
"Hello, hello," he said.
"I want to kiss him,
I want to kiss the baby,
I want to kiss him
SO MUCH!"

And he put the baby
on his shoulders,
and it felt shaky, shaky.
He flip-flap him over
till he nearly drop him.
"Aieeeeee!"

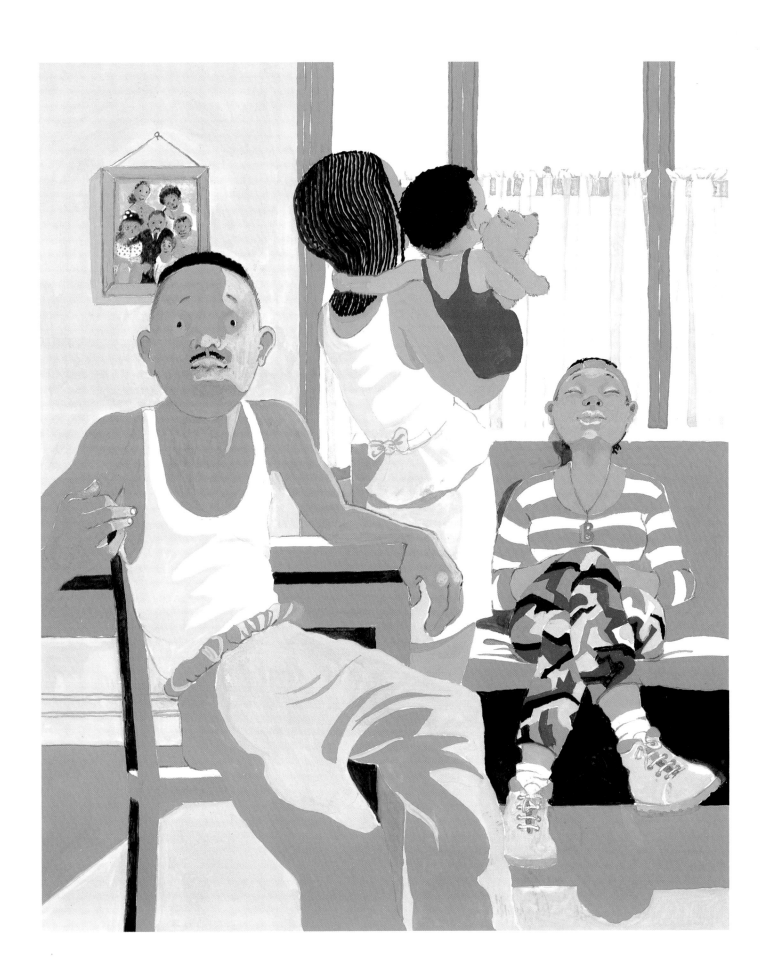

They weren't doing anything,
Mom and the baby and
Auntie Bibba and Uncle Didi,
nothing really . . .

Then,
DING DONG!
"Yoooooo hoooooo!
Yooooooo hooooooo!"

Mom looked at the door,
Uncle Didi looked at Auntie Bibba,
Auntie Bibba looked at the baby,
the baby looked at Mom.
It was . . .

Nannie—
Nannie and Gran-Gran.
Nannie and Gran-Gran came inside
with their handbags cock up
to one side and their 'brella hook up
on their sleeve.
"Yoooooo hoooooo!
Yoooooo hoooooo!" they said.

"I want to eat him,
I want to eat the baby,
I want to eat him
SO MUCH!"

And they hug him
and they love him
and they make him
feel so cozy,
singing songs and dancing
till it was time for sleeping.
"Zzzzzzz . . ."

They weren't doing anything,
Mom and the baby and Auntie Bibba
and Uncle Didi and Nannie
and Gran-Gran,
nothing really . . .

Then,
DING DONG!
"Hey, pow, pow!"

Mom looked at the door,
Nannie looked at Gran-Gran,
Gran-Gran looked at Uncle Didi,
Uncle Didi looked at Auntie Bibba,
Auntie Bibba looked at the baby.
It was . . .

Cousin—
Cousin Kay-Kay (and Big Cousin Ross).
Cousin Kay-Kay came inside
and he spin up his hat
round and round
and he do like he riding horsey,
giddy-up, giddy-up.

"Hey, pow, pow!" he said.
"I want to fight him,
I want to fight the baby,
I want to fight him
SO MUCH!"

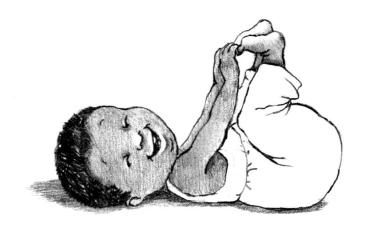

And they wrestle
and they wrestle.
He push the baby first,
the baby hit him back.
He give the baby pinch,
the baby give him slap.
And then they laugh
and laugh and laugh.
"Huh huh huh!"

And the house was full, full, full,
and they sit down there
waiting for the next
DING DONG!
They wait and they wait
but it never come.
Mom said, "Is everybody all right?"
and the baby and
Cousin start to fight again,
Nannie and Gran-Gran
take out cards and dominoes,
Uncle Didi start to slap
them down on the table,
and Auntie Bibba play
some records really loud.
Mom said, "What craziness all around!"

They weren't doing anything,
Mom and the baby and Auntie Bibba
and Uncle Didi and Nannie and
Gran-Gran and Cousin Kay-Kay,
nothing really . . .

Then,
DING DONG!

"I'm home!"
and everybody stopped.
Mom picked the baby up
and they all wait by the door . . .

"SURPRISE!"
everybody said,
and Mom said,
"HAPPY BIRTHDAY, DADDY!"
and everybody joined in.

Then Daddy rub the baby face
against the whiskers on his chin,
and Mom brought in the food
that she'd been cooking . . .

Everybody enjoyed the party.

And when it was time
for them to go
and everybody tired . . .
the baby wanted to play
some more.
Mom said, "No!"
She put him to bed,
but . . .

the baby played
bounce-bounce with Ted,
played bounce-bounce in his crib,
and he remembered
everybody saying
how they wanted
to SQUEEZE
and KISS
and EAT
and FIGHT him . . .

because they loved him
SO MUCH!